NODDY™

Noddy's Perfect Job

D0996815

HarperCollins *Children's Books*

Noddy woke up in his little House-For-One and looked around. Through the window he could see his red and yellow car.

"I don't want to drive my taxi today," thought Noddy. "I would like to try something new." Just then, Master Tubby Bear arrived at his house.

"Hello," called Tubby Bear. "Can I come for a drive with you today, Noddy?"

"I want to try a different job today, Tubby Bear," replied Noddy. "But I don't know what."

"You could try Dinah Doll's stall," said Noddy's friend. "She is having a spring clean and might need some help."

Noddy went straight to Dinah Doll's stall in Toy Town.

"Hello," said Dinah Doll. "What are you up to today?"

"Hello, Dinah," replied Noddy. "I'm bored of driving my taxi. Could I help you spring clean your stall?"

Dinah Doll was very happy to have Noddy help on her stall. She agreed to pay him a few coins everyday.

His first job was to help Dinah paint her stall.

"Wow," thought Noddy, "this is much more fun than driving my taxi."

Because Noddy was so good he decided to save some of his pay each day so he could buy some flowers for Dinah Doll to say thank you. But after three days all the spring cleaning was finished.

"Why don't you go and see if Mr Sparks has any work for you at his garage?" suggested Dinah Doll.

Noddy ran around to Mr Sparks' garage.

"Yes, you can come and clean cars for me," said Mr Sparks. "I am very busy just now and there is a lot of work to do."

Noddy really liked working at the garage. He enjoyed polishing the cars, filling them up with petrol and driving them back to their owners. He enjoyed it so much he even began to miss his own little taxi.

Noddy worked at Mr Sparks' garage for a whole week. But one day Mr Sparks told Noddy that he had worked so hard there was no more work for him to do and he would have to leave. Noddy was very sad and he thought about how he would earn more money. He was thinking so hard he left his bag of coins at the garage.

That night, Noddy went back to fetch his money from the garage. He noticed that the door was open. Suddenly, Sly came roaring past in one of the cars being mended at the garage, followed by Gobbo in another.

"Oh, no!" cried Noddy. "What shall I do?" Noddy jumped onto an old bike and followed the Goblins into the Dark Woods.

He went quite a long way before something dreadful happened - one of the wheels fell off his bike.

"Bump!"

Noddy couldn't go any further.

"Oh, what will I do!" wailed Noddy.

"Who's that? Who's there?" called a voice from the dark. Noddy jumped.
But it was only his friend Big-Ears.
Noddy told Big-Ears everything that had happened to him that night.

"Don't worry," said Big-Ears. "Come back to my house tonight and in the morning we will go and tell Mr Sparks exactly where his cars are. Those naughty Goblins will have hidden the cars deep in the Dark Woods."

In the morning Big-Ears decided to take a walk into the Dark Woods to see if he could find out exactly where Sly and Gobbo had hidden the cars. He soon overheard the naughty Goblins boasting about what they had done. Big-Ears followed them straight to the cars. They were down an enormous rabbit hole by the big oak tree.

Big-Ears hurried to find Noddy and they both rushed off to Mr Sparks' garage. When Noddy got there he got a nasty shock. Mr Plod, the policeman, arrested him!

Everybody thought Noddy had stolen the cars because they found his bag of money in the garage!

"Bang, bang, bang!" Big-Ears was knocking furiously at Mr Plod's police station door.

"Now what's all this?" asked Mr Plod. Big-Ears very quickly told Mr Plod and Mr Sparks about the Goblins stealing the cars and how brave Noddy had been to follow them.

"We should give Noddy a reward for finding the cars!" cried Mr Sparks. "I will give Noddy anything he wants, I just want my cars back."

Mr Plod and Mr Sparks opened the jail and apologised to Noddy for arresting him and thinking that he had stolen the cars.

"I'm very sorry that I broke your bike, Mr Sparks," said Noddy.

"Don't worry, Noddy," said Mr Sparks, kindly. "Can you tell me where the cars are hidden? I have a reward for you."

"Oh, I don't want a reward," replied Noddy. "Big-Ears knows where the cars are."

"The cars are in the Dark Woods in a large rabbit hole by the big oak tree," Big-Ears told them.

Everybody rushed to the Dark Woods. Mr Plod stopped Sly and Gobbo and asked them to tell him where the cars were hidden. But they wouldn't tell.

"Then take me to the rabbit hole by the big oak tree," said Mr Plod.
They took Mr Plod to the big oak tree and there were Mr Sparks' cars.

"Well," asked Mr Plod. "Do you have anything to say for yourselves?"

The Goblins apologised and Mr Plod fined them one bag of gold coins each for stealing the cars.

Mr Sparks got into one car and Mr Plod got into the other, and they drove back to Toy Town.

Noddy and Big-Ears began to walk back to Toy Town. Noddy was thinking about everything that had happened to him in the past few days.

"I have missed driving," he told Big-Ears. "It's a lovely feeling. I think that I will go back to driving my taxi tomorrow. I miss speaking to all my friends too, when I drive them around Toy Town."

"Really?" said Big-Ears, and smiled a little secret smile all to himself.

When everyone got back to Toy Town they found a big surprise waiting for them. The news had gone round the town about Noddy's bravery in chasing the Goblins.

There was a big feast prepared in the Town Square for Noddy and his friends. The jellies were wobbling in their dishes alongside plates of sandwiches and enormous ice creams. It really was a wonderful sight!

"**Wow**, this is a lovely reward! Thank you very much Mr Sparks," gasped Noddy.

"Oh, no, Noddy. This isn't your reward," replied Mr Sparks. "Look over there."

Noddy looked. He saw a car - a very little red and yellow car just big enough for two people. It was Noddy's taxi! There was a note on the front:

'To Noddy. He got back our cars so we have taken special care of his!'

Noddy was so happy he leapt into his shiny, polished car.

"Oh, Big-Ears!" cried Noddy. "What a wonderful surprise! I will be so happy to get back to driving my taxi!"

"That's a brilliant idea, Noddy," agreed Big-Ears. "I am sure you will have lots of adventures!"

Join The All New Noddy Club at
www.NODDY.com

Or:
- ★ **By post:** Download the order form from www.noddy.com and send FREEPOST to: Enid Blyton Ltd, FREEPOST RLTG-HZKL-CRKE, PO Box 5646, Brightlingsea, Colchester, CO7 0SE
- ★ **By phone:** Call the Noddy Hotline on 01206 307 999 (Mon – Fri, 9am to 5pm). National rates apply.

Noddy Club Members receive these 4 great gift parcels over a year:

- ★ A Welcome Pack*
- ★ A Giant A4 Birthday Card
- ★ A Huge A4 Christmas Card
- ★ A Noddy Magazine

WORTH £30

Join up and all these goodies are yours for just £13.99 per annum or £34.99 for a fabulous 3 year membership.

* In the Welcome Pack you receive...

- A personal letter from Noddy & colouring sheet

- A beautiful storybook based on the Noddy TV series

- A cute & cuddly Noddy plush toy (25cm/10" high)

- A bumper-sized Noddy colouring book

- A Noddy activity pack

- A personalised membership certificate with a picture to colour in

- Contents correct at time of printing